W9-AXY-339

WESTMINSTER SCHOOLS

Lindsy
Reed

PRESENTED BY

SMYTHE
GAMBRELL
LIBRARY

A friend

Bijou Le Tord

My Grandma Leonie

Bradbury Press · New York

Bradbury Press
An Affiliate of Macmillan, Inc.
866 Third Avenue, New York, N.Y. 10022
Collier Macmillan Canada, Inc.
Printed and bound in Japan

10   9   8   7   6   5   4   3   2   1

The text of this book is set in 16 point ITC Berkeley Oldstyle.
The illustrations are watercolor.

Library of Congress Cataloging-in-Publication Data
Le Tord, Bijou.   My grandma Leonie.
Summary: A child describes all the things she did with
her grandmother and how she felt when her grandmother died.
[1. Grandmothers—Fiction.   2. Death—Fiction]   I. Title.
PZ7.L568My   1987   [E]   86-32656   ISBN 0-02-756490-8

To the memory of my grandmother

I remember
when
my Grandma
Leonie
came to
live with us.

She brought
a small
brown
radio.

We laughed
and listened
to comedy
shows.

We cried
when
Lassie
didn't come home.

We were
scared
when small
alien creatures
landed
on
earth.

My Grandma
Leonie
loved me.

She called me
her little angel.

Sometimes
she asked,
"What time
is it now, please?"

And she said
again, "What
time is it, please?"

She listened
to different
sounds in the
courtyard

and waited
for spring
and birds to
come back.

She watched
for a neighbor
who kept
her window
open wide
all year.

After school
she read me
the evening
news

and played
her radio
for the two
of us.

One day
my Grandma
Leonie
got
sick.

She drank
hot
cocoa.
But she
would not
feel better.

The next morning
she left
for the hospital.

When she didn't
come back at all,
I stared silently
at the sky.

I sat in
her armchair
and closed
my eyes.

If I missed
her too much
I turned on
the radio.

And I thought
how much
she loved me.

3.